# THE MYSTICAL KAWATARO

## SOMETHING SUSPICIOUS,SOMETHING HIDDEN

FIZZA NIGAR

Copyright © Fizza Nigar
All Rights Reserved.

This book has been published with all efforts taken to make the material error-free after the consent of the author. However, the author and the publisher do not assume and hereby disclaim any liability to any party for any loss, damage, or disruption caused by errors or omissions, whether such errors or omissions result from negligence, accident, or any other cause.

While every effort has been made to avoid any mistake or omission, this publication is being sold on the condition and understanding that neither the author nor the publishers or printers would be liable in any manner to any person by reason of any mistake or omission in this publication or for any action taken or omitted to be taken or advice rendered or accepted on the basis of this work. For any defect in printing or binding the publishers will be liable only to replace the defective copy by another copy of this work then available.

Dedicated to my horror fanatic mum and all my horror fanatic readers...

# Contents

# CONTENTS

# PREFACE

My mum and I are a very big fan of all the creepy creatures and thrilling things that are nothing but superficial things. Every Saturday was meant for a horror-based movie with chilly feelings in the heart. Tho we used to cover our eyes for a few minutes when a spine-chilling, creepy creature or scene used to pop right in front of our eyes.. but then no other feeling would be as horrifying as them.

After a few days, I got a pop-up message in my mind to give a workout to my cortex and thalamus for creating a beautiful thriller book, as a result of which is here THE MYSTICAL KAWATARO..

This book is based on a tremendous creature and have tried my best to make this book an interesting one.

# Acknowledgements

This book is a way of blessing from my dear parents, sister, and friends.

I wouldn't have enough support or help if they weren't there and am thankful for them. Allowing one to achieve something you want is probably not found everywhere. But having a few people around you who motivate you to accomplish your goals is a different feeling. I am lucky enough to have those people around me. Tho they might be few, their brightness level is always on a high mode. My mum has always sacrificed her goals and other valuable things only for me. I am a 17-year-old and even today she stands like a strong pillar beside me guiding, protecting, loving, caring, and whatnot. She instilled in me all the basic etiquette and manners in a much more caring way which is very much needed to face the world confidently. I am proud and thankful to be her daughter.

To my precious grandma, who never let me down and was always ready in the kitchen to serve me my basic needs each and every single day.

From taking my troubles to joining me in my bad times, she was always there for me and encouraged me like no one else. Thank you ammy...

To my chipmunk sister, for always being with me in my notorious times and supporting me. Thank you dear...

Thank you to Notion press for accepting and publishing this book of mine and directing it in a proper direction.

Last but not the least, thank you to all my readers for making up your precious time to read this thriller book.

# PROLOGUE

Mrs.Mariana Quinn and Mr. Juan Quinn have been residing in a beautiful maisonette for about two years with their 3 kids who are: Daniela Quinn the eldest daughter, Valeria Quinn the middle one followed by their youngest son Christopher Quinn. Daniela Quinn is an ongoing psychologist and wants to build a career in that field, Valeria is a middle school-going kid and Christopher is a primary school kid. These two kids attend the same nearby school. Mr.Juan is against Daniela's profession as he feels psychologist is not a good profession or a career for a girl to choose but instead chooses to be a child development specialist or a curriculum developer, but Daniela wishes to achieve the same and plans stuff on how to explain her dad with some proofs. Mrs. Mariana is an arrogant and rude politician but when it comes to her family she is the sweetest of all whereas Mr. Juan is hardworking and short-tempered and works in a shipbuilding company. Just next to their maisonette lies another small maisonette where a family of 4 named the Caleb family has been recently shifted and also are the new neighbors of the Quinn family. Before them, a young couple used to reside there who went bankrupt and had to flee away. This was the reason overheard by Mrs.Mariana by the other neighbors in the town. The Caleb family consisted of Mrs. Savannah Caleb(mother), Mr.Agustin Caleb(father), Matias Caleb(college student), and Gabriel Caleb(primary- kid). Mrs. Savannah is a housewife whereas Mr.Agustin also works in a ship-building company. For about two weeks there was no communication between the Quinns family and Calebs family since they were new and obviuosly takes some time to become familiar with each of them.

# I

# THE BEGINNING...

After a month of holidays, the kids were back to school, the parents started working their respectful jobs, finally all were busy. When Valeria and Christopher stepped out of their gate they noticed Gabriel with the same uniform as theirs and also moving in the same direction to their school. Both assumed that he was studying in the same school but at first they kept quiet as they were not sure if they were right but as soon as they realised that he belonged to the same school Christoper was amazed and ran after him in joy. Valeria could understand the situation and let him go. Gabriel was a plumpy and a happy kid and loved to make friends. On seeing Christopher he felt happy and became a friend of him within a fraction of seconds. Of course kids await to tell their parents their new friends in the same neighbourhood and so were these kids. Their parents were delighted on hearing this news and Mrs. Savannah immediatly walked up straight with a basket of freshly made toasted croissants to meet the Quinn's family. Since both the parents were working, there were only kids in the house. On seeing this she placed the basket with at their entrance and left. In the evening when house was full she again visited the house and now the Caleb's home was empty as gabriel too joined the meeting with his mother.

When they were in the neighbouring house, a strange noise came from the compound. When Mrs.Savannah felt suspicious she went out to check and found a brownish white skull with a arrow head stuck between the two eye sockets. At once she was shooked on seeing this and then went on rounds as a detective, assuming that someone is playing up. Christopher on the other hand started crying and on being asked he said in a low voice " I felt something worried". Daniela brought a fresh croissant that Mrs. Savannah had baked. When there was no crowd around him he stood up from his place, snatched a click pen and started ticking his right forehead. This went about for 10 minutes and then he stopped and went to sleep. Next day morning Mrs.Mariana found 3 alike skulls same as that in their neighbors compound but with a femur bone with greek text inscribed on it. She was shook n felt something weird not paying much importance to the text. She immediatly wore gloves and collected those stuff, dug a ground n hid those under it. As usual the routine was on and she hid the skull story from her husband, Mr.Juan. The kids were back from school n lined up to shower one by one, now it was Christopher's turn and as soon as he poured water starting from the head he immediatly mourned out "Aooooch".. of pain not realising that his right forehead and his right leg was bruised and was swollen. He neither showed up to his mother or his siblings and pretended as if nothing happened to him but the pain was internally paining him dreadfully.

The next day Daniela was heading off to Austria for her further studies in pyschology, she only informed her mother and her siblings about this n not to her dad because she knew he would not allow her so she said," if dad questions on me, tell him that i have gone a educational trip n will return after 3 days". Her mother nodded her head and wished good luck on her journey. Her sister wished for some gifts while returning but Christopher innocently looked on to her and hugged her. He was not in a happy mood, Daniella willingly agreed to them and left.

• 3 •

# II

# THE RANDOM MAGICIAN

Mrs. Mariana was getting worried day by day by encountering those skulls and wanted to share this with someone, as a result of this she stayed at home n went to a nearby library to see if she could find some clues or hints on it. Daniella had just reached Vienna and was all ready for her classes and also to roam around the new place. The kids went home as usual and on their way back home Valeria noticed Christopher dull and questioned him. He answered right away "today am tired and have got a lot of homework to do..", Valeria helped him with his bag and promised to help him with his work too. As they were about to reach their respective houses, Mrs. Savannah yelled out" cum up here ninos, I know you guys are tired so I have made some cheesy tortillas, first enjoy that n then do the rest". The kids ran up except Valeria as she wanted to enjoy her delicious snack after throwing her heavy-loaded bag in her house. As she ran up the case she noticed a brownish metal key lying on the ground. She immediately took it up n thought her mum would have dropped it down here.

Later, at night when everyone was at their respective homes Christopher was sitting on the case corner as if he was deep into some thought and trying to sort out the matter. The next morning, Gabriel was in a hurry to meet Christopher and Valeria. When he met them he said in a happy tone," I have got 3 tickets to a big fair in the nearby town n its stated that all the children in the town are invited, so we have to attend that today at 5 PM at any cost. Valeria, as well as Christopher, was also very excited and we're waiting for the right time to come. The kids informed their mothers and went hurriedly. There was a magic show held for the children so the kids attended the show. The magician seemed to look a bit old, suspicious. He did all the tricks on the kids and not even a single trick on material things. The way he tricked up things seemed as if he was waiting for something but since all the kids were innocent, it was an advantage for him to go about with it. In this trick, he shouted," whoever wants to get a small precious gift, please raise your hand. The first hand will be pulled out.." As soon as all the kids heard this, a small, skinny hand stood up and it was Christopher's hand. He was called onto the stage and was asked to close his eyes and sit on his legs. He did what was asked and the magician covered his eyes with a violet color cloth, kept his magical stick on Christopher's eyes, and uttered"**babrikadiapa yucharava..**", for the first few seconds nothing happened and then Christopher rubbed his eyes harshly. Nothing happened to him but then he was still rubbing his eyes and as a result, they became red. He was then asked to go back to his seat and as promised he gave a small guinea pig. The fair was over and the kids were returning back to their respective homes.

಄

The next morning, Christopher's eyes were red and swollen. He didn't attend a school that day as well as the next three days. Each day the eye got bigger and bigger, whoever attended their house or whenever he went out to play with his friends, and relatives made weird faces while looking at his eye as it had become so worst and creepy. He even grew weaker everyday. His mother and Valeria worried day by day and tried finding out some homemade solutions to it. Since he had no one to talk with, he started sharing his feelings to his guinea pig everyday. Valeria and Gabriel also felt lonely as they were missing out Christopher. Mrs. Savannah came to check on Christopher with a basket full of delicious fruits and after seeing his condition, she felt bad and suggested some ice dipped in honey to be kept on his eyes as it will help his eyes. Mrs. Mariana went according to her and as she was on her way to Christopher's room, she heard Christopher talking to someone and was puzzled. There was no one in the house except her and Christopher. As she went near his room, she heard him saying " I am tired of this and can't take it anymore". She opened the door quickly to find out who was in there but couldn't find anyone and asked Christopher who he was talking to. He replied saying no one and was talking to himself. His mother cared him, made him lie on a bed and started keeping ice on his eyes and gave him some broth after which he slept on his mothers lap.

# III

# VISITING THE DOC !!

Mrs. Mariana lay ill on the bed with mixed emotions and feelings. Christopher on the other side was growing weaker day by day. Valeria was waiting for her father and Daniela to come home as she was all alone and to help her mum, she started doing some household work. She also stopped playing out with Gabriel. Today, after a month, Mr. Juan returned home with a sad, gloomy face. Valeria opened the door and her father's presence made her day a bit ok. As soon as she opened the door and saw her dad, she hugged him tightly. Mr. Juan started searching for the rest of the family. Valeria told him that her mother and Christopher are ill and are lying on the bed and Daniela has gone on an educational trip for three days. Mr. Juan got worried and immediately left to see them. Christopher was sleeping and Mrs. Mariana was reading a novel when Mr. Juan entered their room and hugged his wife. A warm feeling aroused in the room. Half an hour later when Christopher woke up, he saw his dad after a long time and hugged him even though he was weak. On seeing Christopher in this condition, his dad felt bad and started questioning his wife about his health. His wife was clueless on his health. Valeria was doubting the magician for her brother's health. She didn't tell her dad about this as she knew he would shout at her mother for letting them out and also give some strict punishments to the kids. Mr. Juan decided to take him to a nearby centro hospitalario. Mrs Mariana dressed Christopher in a warm chaqueton with a pair of gloves and strong warm thigh high boots. Christopher looked like a porcelain doll. Mr. Juan was ready with his car..

To make him feel better, his dad stopped his car near a streetside toy store and bought him a big ruddy bright eyed teddy. Christopher felt very happy on seeing the teddy and hugged it whole heartedly. After about an hours drive they reached the centro hospitalaria. Mr. Juan carried Christopher in his arms and went straight to the consultants room. Christopher was getting scared entering the doctor's room as he thought they would treat him with long, sharp needles. On seeing Christopher's behaviour, the doctor offered him a small huesito. Christopher didn't take those as he thought that was the way of changing his mind for a few seconds and then inserting that needle in him. But suddenly the doctor said," there is no need for you to get scared from me, as am not treating you with needles". After listening to this Christopher felt a feeling of satisfaction in his heart and immediatly accepted the Huesito. Mr.Juan started explaining the problem to the doctor meanwhile the doctor was examining Christopher. In the end, the doc prescribed a few medications that must be given to Christopher for a period of 7 days.

While returning back home Christopher saw a bunch of green cucmbers on the streetside market and demanded them. Mr.Juan couldn't understand why he wanted them and on pleading him he bought a few fresh green cucumbers for him.

# IV
# ENCOUNTERING THE LOVERS..

It was the month of October and Daniela was working hard in Austria and also enjoying her trip. She made many friends in there. Among them was Matias caleb. Matias was a tall, smart and good looking person. He was very reserved. Daniela used to spend a lot of time with Matias completing their research papers together, attending classess together and so on. On knowing more about Matias she came to know that they live in Spain. Now they got even more close as they belonged to the same country and Daniela felt good as she had someone of her own country. As Matias spent time with Daniela, his heart started developing a different feeling towards Daniela. It was the winter season in Austria then, so Daniela planned to dine out after classes with friends. It was a pleasant evening as it started to snow. Daniela just loved the snow and to make that feeling even more cheerfull she started the game of snowball fight with her friends. The snow was so cold and soft that it gave them shivers whenever they held the snow. Everyone were amazed by the beauty of snow. It looked like an angel, fluttering down from the sky with such grace and elegance and behaving as a white blanket covering the trees, ground and house.

The very next day Daniela fell ill as a result she decided to take a day off from classes and stay in her room. Usually Daniela and Matias attend classes together and leave together, but today since she was unwell Matias went alone. The classes were over and Matias decided to visit Daniela, so he hurriedly ran to her room. As he went up to her room, he found the door latched and locked. As he was worrying and wondering about Daniela, she just popped up in front of Matias after taking a short walk in the nearby park. On seeing that Matias asked Daniela in a very worried tone," Where have you been all the day that too wid such a cold'. Daniela couldn't understand why Matias spoke in such a way and replied,"Its just a normal cold, there is nothing to get worried about it.. and also are you okay? ."Ah..well am not because you are not okay" said Matias. Daniela found this in a very funny way and started laughing uncontrollably. Matias was actually serious about this and the way she laughed made him upset. To make him feel better, she immediatly took out a caramel croissant from her bag and gave it to him as a treat. Matias didn't want to take it but after Daniela apologised him he snatched the treat from her and took a big bite of it.

Matias adored Daniela and had fallen for her completely and didn't know how Daniela could react on knowing this. He thought she would alienate him on knowing this and was cross puzzled. He had sleepless nights and was nervous. He was just waiting for the appropriate time to approach.

# V

# THE UNEXPECTED COMPORTAMIENTO..

Mr. Juan stayed at home taking care of Christopher. Mr. Agustin had also returned back from his work. Valeria and her mother had been out to library giving a fake reason to Mr. Juan. Today Gabriel wanted to visit his close friend. He took some caramel croissants with him as they were its dearest treats and could make him happy.

After greeting Christopher, when he treated him wid croissants, he immediatly threw them away and masticated a part of Gabriel's hand. Mr.Juan was astonished seeing his behaviour and separated both from that act. Later, Gabriel headed towards his home with his eyes filled with tears. Mr.Juan asked him why did he behave in such a way and scolded at him. He replied stating that he doesn't like any other treats other than cucmbers. Mr. Juan was just annoyed with his behaviour and ran behind Gabriel to console him. Christopher's eyes had turned triangular and elongated. His physical features were not the same as before. Valeria and her mum were back from their work and as they were entering their maisonette they found Christopher sitting in a ankle crossed position right in front of few delicious croissants and on the other Mr.Juan consoling Gabriel. Christopher on seeing his mother started yelling for cucmbers.

As soon as he started yelling, the rest of the members of the Caleb's family came running out and on seeing Gabriel weeping, they started questioning him. Gabriel ran inside the home just to hide what Christopher had done to him. He didn't open up to anyone except to Valeria who came later on to ask on him. The mark on the hand was covered with a patch of algodon as it bleeded.

Mr.Juan explained the entire act to his wife which occured during her absence. They got really worried and decided to have a session with Christopher. Mr. Juan spoke in a very aggressive tone. After the session was over, both the parents found him to be very puzzled and also changed. He had developed a liking for green and juicy cucmbers only. Mrs. Mariana gave him some cucmbers which she had bought on her way and put him to sleep. Around 4 AM, Mrs. Mariana was disturbed by some noise in her room. To find out what the noise was, as soon as she arised from her bed, she found Mr. Juan missing. She was puzzled and immediatly ran to Christopher's room to check whether he was with him. But unfortunately, he wasn't there.

It was around 6 in the morning when she was still searching for him untill she met Mr. Agustin who was woodcutting. She went to him and asked him whether he had been with him or seen him. He was clueless of what she was talking to him and replied by no. After understanding what she meant, he joined with Mrs. Mariana in search of him. Later they decided to inform the cops about this act and since she was the politician a greater attention was given to her.

After around two to three hours, when Valeria woke up, she found a titanium watch lying next to Christopher. Valeria was unaware of what was happening in her family and also tried searching for her parents. She tried asking Christopher about the same but he was unresponsive. She later grabbed the watch put it inside her pocket and rushed to her neighbours house. Mrs. Savannah was laying the breakfast table along with Gabriel with his injured hand. Valeria greeted both and then questioned about her parents. Mrs. Savannah broke her question and replied straight away," Dont worry estimado, your mama has gone in search of your dada..". After listening to this, she went to her house. On returning she found a two feet footmark. It was not a normal footmark but looked like big version of duck feet mark. She immediatly called out to Mrs. Savannah. She was surprised on seeing this as it was new to her and immediatly ran for getting her camera to capture these.

# VI
# REVEALING THE SECRET..

It was the fourth day since Mr.Juan had been missing. Mrs. Mariana was terribly broken from inside and couldn't understand what was going with her family. Mrs. Savannah helped her with their daily meals and supported Mariana to not lose hopes. Valeria's grades had also gone down and decided to quit school. Christopher was growing vigorous day by day and ate tons of cucmbers. Everyone wanted to stay away from him. No one knew the exact reason of what was happening to him. If anyone in the family didn't get him any cucmbers then he used to take a big bite of flesh from their hand or chest. Christopher's hand and feet changed. Its webs became prominent, his nose became more narrow and most importantly his body started developing scales of dark green colour with its inside filled with light green patch. He changed his room from bed to a water sauna. Mrs. Mariana was horror struck on seeing him. She wanted someone to be with her at that moment especially her husband but since he wasn't there she immediatly told Valeria to call for Mrs. Savannah.

Mrs. Savannah came running to Mrs. Mariana and when she saw Christopher, she was frightened and stayed away from him.

The only idea that popped in her mind was to visit the library and search for what Christopher had become. Mrs. Mariana then locked Christopher in his room with a few cucmbers and left to the nearby library. On reaching there she immediatly took out some research books on creatures and hybrids. After searching over 9-12 books she found a book whose cover page was similar to Christopher. She skipped the first two pages of the book and then on the third page she found a picture under which it was detailed. It said,".... these creatures are found only in districts of Japan . It has no treatment as such but its weaknesss can be controlled."

Mrs. Mariana purchased the book so that it could be useful for some cases. On her way back home, she was engrossed in her thoughts of what had happened to Christopher and her husband. She was deciding to have a visit to japan so that Christopher could be treated. As she was driving, a two headed monstrous creature just appeared in front of her and broke her front windscreen glass. Mrs. Mariana was severly injured with all the glass pieces entangled on her head and hands.

# VII

# WHAT!......HOW DID THIS HAPPEN?

Christopher was locked up in the spare room and ate of tons of cucmbers. Valeria stayed away from him and used to pass his food through the pet flap below the door. Mrs. Mariana's little finger had been cut off during the incident. Valeria looked after her mum really well. She learnt to cook the basic meals, do the household work, change her mums dressing day to day. Though everyone had hopes that Mrs. Mariana would turn well but she grew weaker everyday which was not a healthy sign. She could not even move a little and stayed resting on her bed all day long wishing to see her family back.

Valeria found a letter lying on the entrance of her maisonette gate. She picked it up right away and showed it to her mother. It was her husbands letter. Mr. Juan had got an venturing offer to continue his work in tokyo and had to leave the place after two days. Mrs. Mariana sighed while folding the letter and visualized Mr. Juan's presence next to her. She got the warm feelings and emotions which she used to get when he was around her. As she closed her eyes, she was reminded by her fondest memory. It was the day they were getting hitched together. Just before a few hours, Mr Juan proposed her with a beautiful diamond ring and promised to stay for each other and together.

As she was in her own memory, there was a hard knock on the front door. On opening the door, Valeria was surprised to see the cops. The cops were here to inform the dreadful news of her father. Since Valeria was a kid, the cops asked for her mother and on knowing that she was unwell, Both the cops entered Mrs Mariana's room to inform the news. Mrs Mariana got some hopes seeing those cops as she thought the cops had brought her husband back. When the cops saw Mrs Mariana so weak and tired, they didn't fell like informing the dreadful news as they thought her health might grow even more weaker. But unfortuantely they had to tell the news. After thinking for few minutes the first cop blurted," miss, this is to inform you that Mr Juan has been slaughtered by a creature. Mrs Mariana fell upon her bed dumbstruck whispering WHAT?. Valeria burst into tears on listening about her father's death. The cops then showed them the bloody stuff of Mr. Juan's during the incident and left.

Mrs Mariana was not in her senses and Valeria tried consoling her mother but she wasn't responding to her. It was a gloomy day and black clouds covered the entire sky.

Early in the morning at around 4:30 AM, Mrs Mariana lay dead on her bed with her hand wrapping her dead husband's frame near her chest.

# VIII
## YESSSS! I DID IT..

The assesments were on and Daniela was on the edge of becoming a proper pyscologist. Matias's training was still on for Psychotherapist. Both had similar intention but in a different way. As Daniela's training and assesments were coming to an end she thought to make a visit to her hometown and meet her family and friends. Before that she had to complete and fulfill her siblings wishlist and for that, she decided to go for shopping in the eve with Matias. Matias was still struggling to open up to her and whenever Daniela used to be with him or around him, he just couldn't talk or make an eye contact with her in a proper way. But today, he decided to open up to her at any cost. At around 5 in the eve, Matias was on his bed thinking on how to tell out to her, when Daniela knocked at his room door. He very well knew that she was at the door and on knowing that he opened the door. Daniela looked hurry and just splurted out few words stating to be ready for shopping with her. Matias couldn't understand a single word of her and asked what was she trying to say. Daniela just sighed at him and repeated what she said. After listening to her, Matias thought this was the chance to let his feelings out to her and willingly agreed to her. Daniela got ready with her shopping list meanwhile Matias was getting ready.

During the shopping hours, Matias asked Daniela whether they could have their dinner out as he had no interest for having the same old porridge in the room. This was actually the way to open up the feelings to her and Daniela willingly agreed to him. Matias got a feeling of satisfaction on listening to her. Just opposite to the shopping mall was a small and a beautiful florist shop. Matias decided to purchase a beautiful scented rose for Daniela as this was the small token for his love to her. He then faked out a reason to Daniela for his absence and made his way to the florist shop. He somehow managed to hide the rose from Daniela throughout the shopping journey.

After about four hours of continous shopping, Matias and Daniela were very very tired. Matias had lost the energy to even stand but after seeing the fresh rose, he got his hopes back. He then invited Daniela to a classy, regional and an elegant restaurant. He acted in such a way that the restaurant belonged to him and Daniela was puzzled with his actions and language. She didn't know the surprise that was waiting for her. Matias then asked the management to reserve a table for two.

After settling down, he asked what Daniela would like to eat, an ordered it. He was nervous before proposing Daniela and didn't know how would she react. He pulled out the strand of rose from his inner pocket of jacket and offered it to Daniela while explaining his feelings to her. Daniela was shook and blushed on seeing this act but didn't utter a single word to Matias.

# IX

# THE SAD ARRIVAL!

Valeria was heart broken. She was now a orphan untill Daniela returned home. There was no one who she could convey her emotions to. Mrs. Savannah took care of her like her own daughter. But Valeria missed her parents comfortment. Now it was all about Christopher. The caleb's family disliked taking care of him due to his physical traits. Even Valeria stopped feeding him as she thought Christopher was the one behind her parents death.

To Valeria's surprise Daniela just returned to her home town with Matias. Little did Daniela knew that Matias resided next to her Maisonette and were neighbours. As Daniela was heading up to her place, she saw Matias following her just behind her. She stopped on her way and asked Matias as to why he was following her. Matias replied that his family had recently shifted to a beautiful maisonette. Daniela immediatly blurted that she was his neighbour. Matias felt even more happier. On reaching their places, Matias saw his dad woodcutting and Gabriel helping his mum in some gardening whereas Daniela saw none. She thought that they might be resting. Mr.Agustin waved at both the kids as he saw them reaching. Daniela had just reached and when she went inside she only found Valeria lying near a wall with her hands covering her head. She called out her name and on listening this, Valeria was initially surprised and then, on turning her head backwards she saw her sister and came running to her. She started weeping while hugging Daniela. Daniela on the other hand couldn't understand what was happening to her and started consoling her. Daniela, while hugging and consoling Valeria started searching for her parents and most importantly Christopher as he was the youngest in the family. After wiping Valeria's tears, she patiently asked her about everyone. Valeria didn't utter a word about Christopher as she wanted to show him directly. Seeing Christopher, Daniela widened her eyes and was literally lost. She couldn't believe that it was her same little brother. She wanted to meet him but valeria stopped her from doing so and warned her with the reason. Daniela went near Christopher and assured him that she would help him in treating him and also doing whatever was possible. She then questioned about her parents and on knowing that they were dead she wept and wept and wept the whole day with a guilt in her heart that she couldn' t meet her parents during their last times. She was feeling very guilty for her father as took him in a wrong way. Daniela hated her father only because he didn't support and agree to her choices and now she was suffering in the most hurtful way. She had totally forgotten about her trip and gifts and instead was fully drenched with the emotion erupting out of her.

# X

# A NEW BEGINNING..

Daniela was a counsellor now. She had too many responsibilties on her and was trying to make arrangements to treat Christopher in the city of tokyo, which she got to know from her mother's book. Valeria continued her primary studies and obeyed her sister respectfully. Matias helped Daniela whenever she required some help. Daniela had two tasks. One was to treat Christopher in tokyo and the other was to find out the hidden mystery behind her dad's death.

Finally Daniela got the chance to visit the city of tokyo, but had a problem in getting Christopher there. He had grown a way to big to carry or get him out. She was also worried that people might get frightened on seeing his presence. She couldn't carry out this plan all by herself and since Matias knew what was going on, she decided to ask Matias for help. Matias willingly agreed to help her out and started their preparation right away.

# XI

# A DELICIOUS MEAL !

It was the cherry blossom festival in tokyo. Thousands of trees burst into bloom, dousing the streets with stunning shades of pink. Daniela, Matias along with Christopher had just reached tokyo- the great city. Daniela was very tired travelling all day long so she decided to have something and was not sure of what to have. Just by this, an old man passed by and Matias stopped him to ask to suggest a hotel or restaurant nearby. Daniela never knew that Matias could speak japanese. After getting the required answer he bowed to him as a token of respect and let him go and returned to Daniela. She looked on to him in a doubtful way and just before she could ask him anything, Matias told her about the place for having their meal. Daniela was not in a mood to fight as she lacked of energy.

Christopher's sara became prominent. As a result of which another old man stopped by and suggested Daniela in his language to leave Christopher in the nearby pond by talking in gestures. As such Daniela couldn't understand anything, Matias nodded his head and thanked the random old man and re explained the enitre content in her language.

There was a small, deep pond just beside an old shimmering tree, and they decided to drop Christopher there while they would find out the ways to treat him.

After leaving Christopher there with some cucmbers, both were back to their journey to the breakfast stall. They walked a mile when they found a small, cute and a classy store. Many people gathered around the store enjoying there delicious meals and both went on to check for a unoccupied table. At last they got a table and ordered for some sushi's, takoyaki and tempura. The meals were scrumptious and the cherry blossoms made their meals taste even more better.

# XII

# THE NOTORIOUS THIEF...

As they got to know more about Christopher, Daniela made quick notes in her special observatory book. She noted the tiniest thing growing or happening to him. After getting much information, they got to know that to treat Christopher, they had to meet a old shinshoku who lived in the shinjuku city which was 15 kilometer away from where they were. They had no other option than to travel by their feet. Of course it would take time to reach that place so decided to rest in a cottage which was in a nearby street.

On their way, they captured many beautiful creations of nature with the help of Matias's camera which belonged to his mother. The cherry blossom weather made Matias felt a bit nappy and thought to take a break by having a good nap of half an hour. Daniela just sighed at his behaviour and conveyed to him in a annoyed tone to wait untill they reached the cottage.

A grey haired man just dashed by Daniela. He was in a hurry and looked as if he was been chased by some cops. Daniela banged her head against the tree bark while Matias ran behind the cops which were behind the grey haired man. Meanwhile Daniela, rubbed her hand against her head and went behind Matias to know what was going on. A samurai got hold of the man from the front.

The man had been under arrest because he used to hypnotise small kids with random magical portion and turn them into various creatures. Daniela immediatly filed a complaint against him stating that he was the one who had turned Christopher in the mystical creature. This mystical creatures name was hidden. With Daniela's request, the cops further interrogated the unknown man about the kids he had met in the past. Daniela and Matias didn't need to have anymore researches as the grey haired man was the one who had turned Christopher in a creature. The originality of the man was a wizard who hated children to the core and made magical portions and changed them thereby leading to creatures. Daniela lay still on the chair and requested the cops to sentence him to death.

# XIII
# LOST AND FOUND!

Daniela was lost in her own thoughts thinking about Christopher. She knew him very well and was confused with the thought. As she was engrossed in her thought,the cops followed her as they had something very urgent to tell them. It was something to show her in some place. After having a converstaion with both, they joined the cops crown. On further being asked, they got to know that the place they were about to reach belonged to the wizard who turned Christopher in a creature.

They had reached their destination. Its place looked like an broken piece of some broken house covered with black. The cops just broke inside the house and Matias and Daniela couldn't believe of who they met. It was Mr. Juan. Daniela thought he had been dead because of whom her mother died. She just couldn't control her emotions and went and hugged her dad. Mr. Juan was very happy on seeing Daniela as he didn't expect her to be there and was in the assumption that he will be left there alone forever.

Just as Daniela went near him, Mr. Juan disguised himself as a vampire. He in reality was a vampire who just waited to for a chance to have Daniela and her mother. He was relieved on knowing that her mother was no more as his burden became less. He then made a wound on her neck whispering a happy journey and sucked her blood. Matias seized a shooter from one of the cops and tried attacking the vampire. But he was too late as a little later Daniela fell dead on Matias's shoulder.

# XIV
## THE LAST KEY..

Mattias was ruptured in pieces and all his upcoming dreams were tore apart. He had totally forgotten that he was a psycotherapist as he couldn't handle himself and acted as sot. But as he wanted to fulfill her last desire, without any delay he headed on his way to meet the old shinshoku by bringing Christopher with him.

After covering a long distance he finally reached the desired place. A beautifully designed minka stood aside a tree showering blossoms. He went inside exploring and observing the amazing architecture along with Christopher. Just beyond the sliding door was a sage in seiza whose long fine hair covered both of his shoulders equally with a chonmage on the top. He looked serious while he was not. Matias bowed to him as a token of respect. The sage invited him in along with Christopher. Matias then explained about the reason being there.

Matias was still explaining as the sage interrupted him. "..he is a kawataro. these have a power of treating humans by manupilating bones and joints and at the same time can also be dangerous by attacking them. Treat them with some chilly cucmbers and they will never forget you."

He then blurted Christopher was surely a mystical Kawataro...

www.ingramcontent.com/pod-product-compliance
Lightning Source LLC
Chambersburg PA
CBHW061408160726

47995CB00002B/516